BIG JABE

For all those, long gone,
who gave help, tried to help, or wanted to help,
and made some lives roll easier—JN

For my parents, grandparents, great-grandparents,
great-great-grandparents . . . —KN

Special thanks to Alice Eley Jones for historical
consultation on the artwork—KN

Watercolor and gouache were used for the full-color illustrations.
The text type is 14-point Aldine 401 BT.

Text copyright © 2000 by Jerdine Nolen

Illustrations copyright © 2000 by Kadir Nelson

Published by Lothrop, Lee & Shepard Books
a division of William Morrow and Company, Inc.
1350 Avenue of the Americas, New York, NY 10019
www.williammorrow.com
Printed in Hong Kong by South China Printing Company (1988) Ltd.
10 9 8 7 6 5 4 3 2

LIBRARY OF CONGRESS CATALOGING-IN-PUBLICATION DATA
Nolen, Jerdine. Big Jabe/by Jerdine Nolen; illustrated by Kadir Nelson.   p. cm.
Summary: Momma Mary tells stories about a special young man who does
wondrous things, especially for the slaves on the Plenty Plantation.
ISBN 0-688-13662-1 (trade)—ISBN 0-688-13663-X (library)
[1. Slavery—Fiction. 2. Afro-Americans—Fiction. 3. Tall tales.] I. Nelson, Kadir, ill.
II. Title. PZ7.N723Bi 2000 [E]-dc21 99-38001 CIP

Jerdine Nolen
BIG JABE

ILLUSTRATIONS BY
Kadir Nelson

LOTHROP, LEE & SHEPARD BOOKS
New York

We have a great big pear tree in our yard, down by the river. Poppa Jabe planted it there in slavery times. That tree doesn't give any fruit now—it's too old. But Momma Mary says that sometimes, after it's gotten a good rest, little white flowers blossom on it in the spring.

"That tree has probably forgotten more of the world than most folks remember," Momma Mary says. And on days when the wind blows in whispers that only bees can hear, she tells me a "long, long time ago" story, like the one about how freedom came to the slaves on the Plenty Plantation.

A long, long time ago, when young Addy was a house slave on Simon Plenty's plantation, she *had* to clean out the Big House. But what she *loved* to clean out was the river. And when she went fishing, she made sure that *everyone* got lots of fish to eat, and not just the heads or tails either.

Now Mr. Plenty loved his catfish, bass, and brim. He loved them baked or poached or cooked all together in a spicy bayou fish stew. But he especially loved them fried just the way Addy's cousin Sweetie Belle fried them.

One day, early in the spring, Mr. Plenty awoke with a powerful hunger for fish—so he sent Addy down to the river to fetch some.

By midday Addy was mighty vexed; she hadn't gotten a single nibble on her line. If her luck didn't change soon, she'd be facing a Mr. Plenty who was both angry *and* hungry. She tried not to think about which was worse.

Then Addy saw something bobbing in the water. It was a wicker basket, and something was inside it.

When the basket got caught in the roots of a fallen tree, Addy ran downstream to catch up to it. A little boy 'bout five or six years old just sat there, smilin' up at her.

She scooped him up and set him on the ground. In the bottom of the basket, where he'd been sitting, was a plump round pear, as golden as the noonday sun.

"Here," said the boy. "For you. For fishing me out of the river."

Addy took a bite and sighed. "This must be the fruit of heaven," she said. "What they call you?"

"Jabe," he told her.

When Addy had finished the pear, Jabe dug a deep hole with a stick, dropped the seeds into it, and covered them over. Then he brought water from the river to soak them.

"They want to grow," he told her.

Well, Addy thought, it *is* spring, after all.

Jabe looked at Addy's fishing poles. Then he looked at her empty wagon.

"You fishin'?"

"S'pose to be, but I ain't catch nary a one."

Jabe leaned over the river, cupped his hands around his mouth, and called:

"Fish, fish, where is you, fish?
Jump to the wagon like Miss Addy wish!"

Suddenly the earth began to tremble, the river began to roil, and the air was filled with fish—jumping, hopping, flying right into Addy's wagon.

Jabe opened his little-boy mouth and laughed a big man-sized laugh.

Mr. Plenty took no notice of Jabe that day; it was hard to see anything over the piles and piles of fish. Come nightfall, with the chores all done and the Big House finally settled and quiet, Sweetie Belle and Addy set out to collect the fish that she and Jabe had hid for the folks in the Quarters. Laying boards atop some barrels, the women-folk set a fine table, and there was no hunger around it *that* night.

Jabe sat next to Addy. "This the first little-boy fish I ever did catch," she said, and laughed. And when she told about the wonderful way Jabe had caught all those fish—"Called 'em right out the water, he did!"—folks ooohed and aaahed, and Jabe sat up tall in his seat.

That spring was the growingest spring anyone on the Plenty Plantation ever remembered. Cotton plumped up so quick, it seemed to blossom overnight. Cornstalks looked to scrape the sky, yielding foot-long ears of sweet, sweet corn. Chicks hatched by the dozen. New foals were ready to saddle break at six months.

Jabe was growing too. By May he'd left his boyhood behind and showed no signs of stopping. By June he was a full-grown man and had the strength of fifty. He could weed a whole field of soybeans before sunup, hoe the back forty by midday, and mend ten miles of fence by sunset. Life in the Quarters just didn't feel so burdensome with Jabe around. Suddenly there was time for leisure. But this enraged Mr. Sorenson, the overseer, just as much as it satisfied the slaves.

Addy spent her evenings at the riverbank, visiting the tree she and Jabe had planted. From night to night, she could hardly believe her eyes. One day it was a sprout, the next it was a sapling, the day after that it was a young tree full of pretty white blossoms to decorate Addy's hair. In another blink of an eye, that tree looked as if it had been rooted there forever. Its mighty trunk made Addy feel safe. She went to it often and stayed with it late. Its branches arched out over her, full of luscious pears. And there, shining between them, the North Star sparkled overhead.

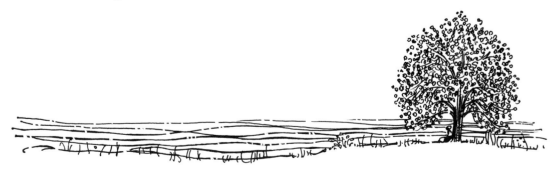

No sooner had the seed leaves appeared than long rows of fluffy white clouds spread over the land. The cotton was ready for harvesting. And Jabe was ready for the cotton. One night, by the light of the moon, he set out alone for the field.

He moved so fast, that field looked like a snowstorm in the dead of winter! So much cotton was flying 'round that come morning, when the sun rose up, it couldn't shine through. So the cock didn't crow. Not an animal in the barn stirred. And not a single person, in the Big House *or* the Quarters, knew that a new day had dawned. Everyone slept late.

By noon Jabe had finished the picking, and the sun finally blazed down on row after row of bags stuffed to overflowing.

It was such a plentiful harvest that no one noticed the sacks Jabe carried off to the Quarters, with enough cotton in them to replace every corn husk in every mattress.

But as the slaves looked forward to the first soft sleep of their lives, Mr. Sorenson was boiling over. With Jabe doing all the work, just who was he supposed to oversee anyway? He aimed to break Jabe, but Mr. Plenty wouldn't hear of it. "I don't want *anything* interfering with Jabe's calling," he said. "You're not to lay a hand on him, you hear?"

So Mr. Sorenson stayed away from Jabe. But when he found Pot-Tim whistling as he worked in the stables, he whupped him good.

It was a good thing for Mr. Plenty that all the cotton was picked, because
the very next morning, a twister blew in bad. It lifted full-grown trees out of
the ground and tossed them around like they were no more than dry leaves.

It picked up the chicken coop, chickens and all, and carried it to the middle of the cow pasture. It tore the roof clean off the barn; not a shingle was left behind. Then that storm stopped, as suddenly as it had started.

Mr. Sorenson sent for Pot-Tim to mend the barn roof, but he was nowhere to be found. Pot-Tim had vanished, and his wife Mollie and their two children with him. Mr. Sorenson was certain they'd escaped under cover of the storm, and he set out with the dogs after them. But the hounds never picked up a scent.

"Twisters startin' to carry *families* off too?" Sweetie Belle mocked behind the overseer's back.

"Sho' nuff strange," Jubal agreed. "Bet they's in Ohio by now!" He chuckled and slapped his knee.

Addy listened to them all and pondered their words in her heart. She thought about the day she'd found Jabe, and how he'd filled her wagon with fish. She thought about how fast every little thing had been growing. And she thought about that pear tree, with the North Star shining through its branches. Suddenly Addy gasped. "Jabe took Pot-Tim to that pear tree," she whispered, but no one heard.

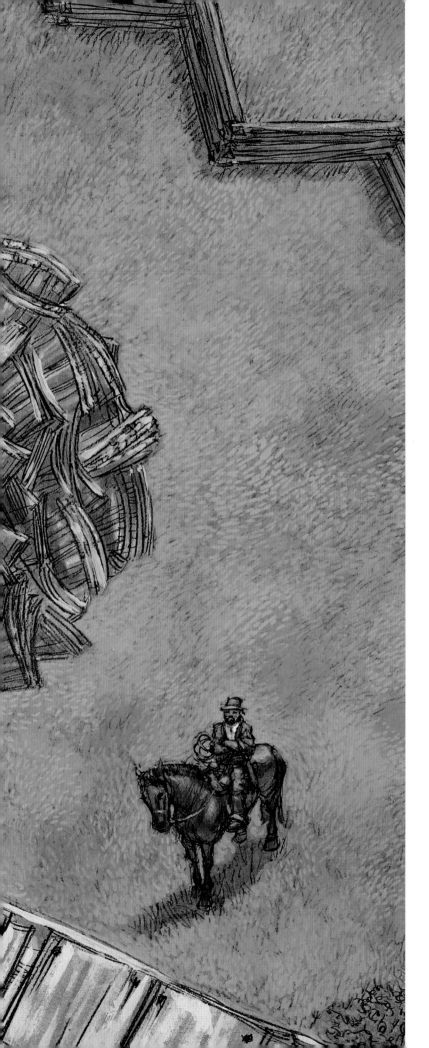

Mr. Sorenson set Jubal and Lester to repairing the barn roof, but Jabe came along with them. How his hammer flew! Seemed like Jubal and Lester never even had to hand him a nail. They tried to help, but truth was, Jabe didn't leave them much to do. The roof was raised long before suppertime, as tight and secure as a drum.

Mr. Sorenson, who'd watched tight-lipped all afternoon, fumed. Though he could find no fault with the roof, and he didn't dare find fault with Jabe, he *could* let loose on Jubal—and he did.

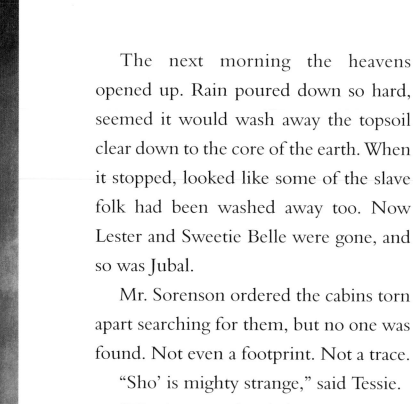

The next morning the heavens opened up. Rain poured down so hard, seemed it would wash away the topsoil clear down to the core of the earth. When it stopped, looked like some of the slave folk had been washed away too. Now Lester and Sweetie Belle were gone, and so was Jubal.

Mr. Sorenson ordered the cabins torn apart searching for them, but no one was found. Not even a footprint. Not a trace.

"Sho' is mighty strange," said Tessie.

"Wasn't no wind took *them* away," Hazel added.

"Weren't no flood, neither." Jim clicked his tongue. "I bet they went the way of the river, and water washed their footprints away!"

"Naw," said George. "River runs south, and it runs too fast to follow nohow."

"Maybe Moses come in the night . . . ," said Mazey.

"Jabe took them to that pear tree," Addy whispered. This time people listened.

But in spite of twisters and floods and missing slaves, the Plenty Plantation was as good as its name that summer.

Speckled cows spotted the fields and gave enough milk to fill a river.

Sheep produced enough wool in one shearing to knit a blanket big enough to cover the entire farm.

The barn was bursting at its seams.

Three more smokehouses had to be built to handle all the meat.

The larder in the Big House was crammed so full, Addy could hardly open the door to stuff in more.

Then came the day when Susie, a broken-down old plow horse, was to be put down. But when Mr. Sorenson went for her, Susie was gone. Folks thought she had walked off to die on her own, but she turned up that afternoon, grazing beneath the pear tree.

Now, there was nothing so odd about that. What *was* odd was that Susie had got hold of her youth again. She whinnied and pranced like a new foal. Somehow she'd changed from a tired old workhorse into a young filly ready for a race!

It was George who found her and brought her back, and his story spread through the Quarters like fire set to dry kindling. But when Mr. Sorenson asked where she'd been, George just told him, "In the woods."

Mr. Sorenson knew there had to be more to it than that! And he was certain beyond a shadow that Jabe had something to do with it. And who'd brought Jabe to the Plenty Plantation in the first place? Addy, that's who! If there was magic afoot, then Addy had to have *something* to do with it.

Neither Mr. Sorenson *nor* Mr. Plenty wanted anything to do with spells and charms. So Addy was put in chains and locked away in the smokehouse.

"Come morning, I'm selling that gal away from here," said Mr. Plenty.

First thing next morning, Mr. Sorensen went for her. But when he undid the lock and opened the door, the chains were lying empty on the floor. Addy had disappeared!

Mr. Sorensen was fit to be tied. He searched the barn; he searched the Quarters; he searched the Big House; he searched the entire plantation. Then he set out with the dogs. But it was all to no avail. Like the others, she had vanished without a trace.

Some said she *was* magic and had flown out through the smokehouse chimney.

Some said she'd tunneled under the floor and made her escape like any mortal.

But some looked out at Jabe chopping wood and breathed the thought that no one would say aloud: "Jabe took Addy to that pear tree."

After a while, Momma Mary tells me, Jabe moved on. One day he too disappeared from the Plenty Plantation, though he turned up at different times in different places throughout the South. And everywhere he did, burdens were lifted.

Momma Mary tells me all the stories, but the most wonderful, she says, happened right here at our old pear tree. And on days when the wind blows in whispers that only bees can hear, I know that she's right.